Too Much Fun

I wish, I wish
With all *my* heart
To fly with dragons
In a land apart.

A Random House PICTUREBACK® Book
By Carol Pugliano-Martin
Illustrated by The Thompson Bros.
Based on the characters by Ron Rodecker

Random House New York

Text and illustrations copyright © 2002 Sesame Workshop. Dragon Tales logo and characters ™ & © 2002 Sesame Workshop/Columbia TriStar Television Distribution. All rights reserved under International and Pan-American Copyright Conventions. Published in the United States by Random House, Inc., New York, and simultaneously in Canada by Random House of Canada Limited, Toronto, in conjunction with Sesame Workshop. Sesame Workshop and its logos are trademarks and service marks of Sesame Workshop.
Library of Congress Control Number: 2001091436
ISBN: 0-375-81608-9
www.randomhouse.com/kids/sesame
Visit Dragon Tales on the Web at www.dragontales.com
Printed in the United States of America   June 2002   10 9 8 7 6 5 4 3 2 1
PICTUREBACK, RANDOM HOUSE, and the Random House colophon are registered trademarks and the Please Read to Me colophon is a trademark of Random House, Inc.

"Max, look!" cried Emmy as she ran into the playroom. "Mom made cookies! She said we can each have one before dinner."

"Mmm, this is yummy!" Max said, gulping his cookie. "But I wish I could have more!"

Just then, Emmy and Max noticed their magical dragon scale glowing.

"The dragons are calling us!" they shouted.

"Hi, Max. Hi, Emmy," Cassie greeted her friends
when they arrived in Dragon Land. "It's such a beautiful
day, we're having a party to celebrate!"

"We've packed a picnic. Let's go to Dragon Land Park
to eat it," Ord suggested.
"Looove it!" said Wheezie.

Lots of dragons were enjoying the beautiful day along the way to Dragon Land Park.

"Okay, we're here," Max announced when they reached the park. "Let's dig in!"

"Look, Max," said Emmy. "Your favorite—pizza!"

"Wow!" Max said excitedly. "And dragonberry cookies, dragoncorn, and dragonberry cupcakes!"

"And I baked a delicious Dragon Deluxe cake!" said Zak.

Max started with a dragonberry cupcake and moved on to dragoncorn, dragonberry cookies, and then pizza!

"You'd better slow down, Max, or you won't have room to eat anything else," Emmy warned him.

"Especially my Dragon Deluxe cake," said Zak.

"I'm all right," said Max, patting his stomach. "I've got *plenty* of room."

"Gee, Max, you must be hungry. But if you don't take a break, you won't feel so good later," said Cassie.

"Don't worry," Max insisted. "I could eat a whole mountain if I wanted!"

"Come on, Ord. Let's go flying together," Max said after he had finished eating a little bit of everything.

"Sounds great!" said Ord. "You know how I love to fly!"

Max and Ord flew and flew until Ord got tired.

"Come on, Ord. Let's keep going!" said Max.

"Sorry, Max. I'd like to, but I've got to rest," said Ord. "Maybe you should, too."

"Naw, I feel fine," Max said. "I want
to have *more* fun! Who wants to ride the
carousel?"

Emmy, Cassie, and Zak and Wheezie
trooped off with Max for a ride.

The group whirled around and around. Suddenly they heard voices.

"More, more!
We want more!
We always want more.
That's what more is for!"

"Uh-oh," Cassie whispered. "It's the Wantmore Twins."

"Stay away from them," warned Zak. "They're trouble."

"They don't sound like trouble to me," said Max. He joined the twins in chanting:

"*More, more!*
We want more!
We always want more.
That's what more is for!"

By this time, Max's friends were ready to head back.

"Hey, where are you guys going?" Max asked.

"All that spinning made me a little dizzy," said Cassie.

"I think I need to sit down," said Zak.

"Come on, Max," called Emmy. "Aren't you tired yet?"

"I'm fine. You go on ahead," said Max.

"I'm tired of everyone telling me not to have more," Max said to the twins. "Let's ride again and again and again!"

"More, more!
We want more!
We always want more.
That's what more is for!"

Max and the twins rode the carousel ten more times. But all that riding made them very thirsty.

The twins led Max to a river of fizz.

"Wow!" Max shouted. "A whole river of fizz! I'm thirsty enough to drink it all!"

"Now let's ride on the swings!" said the twins, and off they went.

Up and down, up and down, Max and the Wantmore Twins swung and swung.

After a long time on the swings, Max and
the twins still wanted more fun.
"Follow us!" cried the twins.
Max had to run to keep up with them.
"It's a volcano!" shouted Max. He could
hardly believe his eyes.

"But instead of lava, this volcano spouts ice cream!" the twins explained. "Dig in!"

Just as Max started eating, he heard Wheezie calling. "Max, time for the Dragon Deluxe cake!"

"I want more ice cream, but I'm getting kind of full," said Max. "And I do want to save room for Zak's cake."

"Come on, Max," insisted the twins. "You should have more and more. And after that, how about even more?"

Max looked down at his tummy, then up at the volcano, then down at his tummy again. "My tummy's just not big enough!" he said. "I guess sometimes more can be too much, and too much fun is no fun at all. Thanks, anyway."

Max ran back to find his friends.

"Max! You're just in time for the Dragon Deluxe cake!" Wheezie exclaimed. "Here you go, Max." Zak handed Max a piece of cake. "It's our specialty."

"I'm glad I saved some room for this," said Max. "It's yummier than an ice cream volcano!"

"Max, I think it's time to go home," said Emmy.

"I guess you're right," said Max. "Bye, everyone. Thanks for a super picnic!"

Back in their playroom, Max lay down to rest.
"You know, Em, I'm feeling kind of full," he said.
"Emmy, Max, time for dinner," they heard their
mother call.
Max held his tummy. "Uh-oh!" he moaned. Then he
and Emmy looked at each other and burst into giggles.